MW01104080

THE DARK LENS

by Thomas Kingsley Troupe

www.12StoryLibrary.com

12-Story Library is an imprint of Peterson Publishing
Company and Press Room Editions.

Produced for 12-Story Library by Red Line Editorial

Photographs ©: Shutterstock Images, cover, 3

Cover Design: Emily Love

ISBN
978-1-63235-054-1 (hardcover)
978-1-63235-114-2 (paperback)
978-1-62143-095-7 (hosted ebook)

Library of Congress Control Number: 2014937421

Printed in the United States of America
Mankato, MN
June, 2014

CHAPTER
1

You got used to getting mugged, at least that's what Alex Hanes thought. It hadn't happened in about four months, so he wasn't sure he'd like it any more than he did the last time. Even so, he knew the routine. Calmly hand over your stuff, don't make a fuss and keep calm. Pretty easy, really.

There was only that one time when he got punched in the face and called the "n-word." The shot in the mouth was easy to take. Getting nasty on top of it was worse. Even so, he kept cool, didn't make a big stink about it, and pulled the money out of his wallet. That part hurt a bit, too, especially since he was trying to save up for a car.

And so, being a five-time-mugged veteran, Alex still walked to work after school. He didn't have a choice. His mom didn't have a car, and if he hoped to have enough money to buy one by the time he turned 16 next year, he walked to work.

It was the same routine just about every afternoon. He came home, ate a quick frozen burrito, washed it down with some grape Kool-Aid, grabbed his backpack, and hit the streets. Sports and anything else took a backseat. He wanted a car. You didn't get mugged in a car. You got where you were going a lot quicker in a car. Girls liked guys with a car. Car, car, car.

As Alex headed to work that Thursday, he saw a cluster of guys hanging at the corner of Third Street and Portage Avenue. They were older, laughing at something Alex couldn't hear. His head told him to play it safe, so without a second thought he turned down Rankin Avenue and went a block out of his way. He wasn't sure if the guys were some of the thugs who'd mugged him in the past. Alex learned it was better to be safe than sorry.

Keep your head down and keep walking, Mom always told him. *That's how I stayed out of trouble.*

As he rounded the corner to Fourth Street, Alex spotted the run-down and abandoned First Baptist Church in the middle of the block. It sat on a lot overgrown with weeds and littered with empty liquor bottles and fast-food wrappers. The old, stained glass windows were long since removed or smashed out, replaced with warped plywood boards.

Alex heard that addicts had taken over the place and called it their own. Even so, it looked pretty empty to him. It was hard to walk by and not wonder what it had been like when it was still full of people. Or at least people looking to worship.

Alex smelled grilling meat as he walked past the church, followed by the stale smell of liquor mixed with dirt. In front of the church, a section of the sidewalk was covered with mud. Alex watched his step, not wanting to slop up his shoes. As he did, he caught a glint of light near his right foot.

At first Alex thought it was the bottom of a broken bottle, but at second glance it looked . . . different. He peered over his shoulder and up ahead, ever cautious for trouble. Then he squatted down and touched the rounded piece of glass. It was a smoky gray color, cloudy with dirt and grime. Designs were etched around the edges. They were caked with grime, making them illegible. With a tug, Alex pulled the glass free, leaving a small circle in the mud. The smoky glass was heavier than he expected and felt warmer than it should.

"Weird," Alex whispered to himself. He turned the glass in his hand and tried his best to figure out what it was and where it might've come from.

His mom watched shows about people finding antiques and rare stuff, so Alex immediately wondered if he'd found some sort of valuable artifact. With an abandoned napkin he found nearby, he brushed away the dirt and mud as best as he could. For extra cleaning power, he spat on his find, working the grime out of the intricate carvings along the rounded edge of the glass.

When it was mostly clean, Alex thought it looked like a lens. A dark, cloudy lens.

He tilted the lens to illuminate the etchings. A few brightened as the light struck them. A small beam of purplish light refracted from the other end, casting a strange smoky glow on the sidewalk.

What Alex saw next startled him.

As the light beam continued to hit the sidewalk, wisps of grayish-purple smoke rose, leaving the sidewalk changed. The concrete looked altered, covered with cracks and blackened as if burned. When Alex touched the dark spot, it felt the same.

It's like a filter, Alex decided. *You put it over a light and it looks different.* He'd seen the same sort of thing at holiday displays in stores. Some made snowflake shapes or stars or even jack-o'-lanterns.

Certain that's what it was, Alex held up the lens to the October sun. He peered through it, looking for the telltale markings that explained how he'd made the sidewalk look temporarily different.

As he lined up the sun perfectly with the inside of the lens, the etchings along the edge burst into a bright and steady glow. In an instant, Alex's face was bathed in the smoky beam of light.

Suddenly, he was somewhere else.

CHAPTER
2

The world around Alex had changed. Above him the sky turned from blue to an angry, blood-red hue. The sidewalk beneath his feet buckled and split, nearly knocking him to the ground.

Old and proud trees from his neighborhood now appeared twisted and barren of any life. Shadowy creatures lurked in their gnarled branches and peered down at Alex with glowing red eyes. He heard low growls in their throats, as if they were waiting to pounce on him and tear at his flesh.

The air around him was thick and humid, as if fall had become an otherworldly southern summer heat wave. Sweat exploded across his forehead and ran into his eyes, making them sting.

"Where . . . ," Alex mumbled, unable to finish. He looked at the abandoned church and watched it crumble to debris, as if knocked down by some invisible wrecking ball. Chunks of stucco and woodwork splintered as the wreckage shifted. To Alex's horror, a large, gray hand emerged from the rubble, the fingers bloodied and twisted. A moment later, a misshapen head rose. It shook chunks of church away from the pile. One of the fiend's eyes was sewn shut. A torn hole in a canvas of grey flesh was its mouth. Three jagged teeth poked from the awful opening and a white, blistered tongue ran across them.

"Why . . . are . . . you . . . here?" a voice rasped, as the beast freed itself from the church's ruins. Alex's panic rose exponentially. *I have to get out of here,* he thought.

Alex stepped back, his heart turbocharged beneath his ribs. An acrid stink assaulted his nose, and he looked down. His feet were planted in the mushy carcass of a long-dead animal. Maggots animated the sickly meat, covering Alex's shoes. He felt tiny bodies squirm against his exposed ankles.

"Oh my God," Alex whispered. He leapt from the rotten animal and shook his leg, launching maggots from his feet. All around him, nothing looked like it had. The houses were no longer houses but abandoned shacks, where haunted faces watched him from dark and shattered windows.

The shambling corpse stepped out of the church rubble. It was free from the wreckage, limping toward him on a dead, splintered foot. The clothes that still hung from its body were shredded rags, failing to cover the horror beneath.

Something in his hand throbbed. Alex was afraid to look. There, still clutched in his fingers, was the dark lens. He raised the glass up to shatter it to the ground. Maybe then his world would return to normal.

No! a thought inside his head screamed. Alex had another idea.

He scrambled backward as the monster slowly drew near. Something inside its throat gurgled.

With fumbling fingers, Alex raised the lens to the orange-ish sun in the bloody sky. He shakily lined it up again so that it fit perfectly inside the ring of inscriptions.

The light ignited the dark lens and Alex was enveloped in white. He felt the air around him cool. The smell of steaks on a grill met his nostrils, replacing the rot of the other world.

Alex blinked. When his eyes opened, his world was normal again.

As normal as it could be, anyway.

✦ ✦ ✦ ✦ ✦

"You okay, kid?" A shriveled old woman stood farther up the sidewalk, her walker parked in front of her. She wore what looked like a lime green pantsuit and had earmuffs on her ears.

"Yeah, I'm . . . I'm fine," Alex said. His heart continued to thunder inside his chest. He looked down and saw his feet were maggot-free. "I . . . I think so, anyway."

"Where'd you come from?" the woman asked.

Alex didn't say anything, since he didn't know. He glanced at the church. It looked as empty as ever, but it was still standing. There was no sign of the hideous fiend crawling out of the wreckage to get him. Everything was back where it belonged.

Was I hallucinating? Was any of that real?

His sweaty forehead and the dark lens in his hand were his only otherworld souvenirs. The lens no longer throbbed. For reasons he couldn't explain, Alex unslung his backpack, unzipped the back pocket and dropped the lens inside.

Maybe someone, somewhere would pay a lot of money for something like it, he thought.

Car money.

Alex drew a deep breath and managed to smile at the woman as he walked past. He couldn't believe what had just happened. It didn't seem possible. It also didn't seem possible for his heart to beat any faster. He cringed, remembering the horrors he encountered. He checked his shoes again. Still no maggots.

What was that? Alex wondered. *What happened to me?*

* * * * *

"Dude, you're late," Turd said as Alex walked through the front door of the Gas N' Grab convenience store. His disheveled coworker stood behind the counter, staring at his watch like the world's worst boss. The blue vest that was his uniform was dingy and wrinkled. Turd's nametag, which read "Kevin," was crooked.

"I've got a pretty good excuse," Alex said, but then he worried he might have to explain what had happened to him if Turd was actually listening.

"Well, punch in and get up here," Turd said. "I've gotta pee."

Alex nodded as he went into the cramped and cluttered back room. He dropped his backpack down by the small break room table

16

and approached the time clock. Gas N' Grab hadn't upgraded to a new timecard system and still used paper cards that slipped into the clock for stamping. Alex found his just below KEVIN MUSTARD. Knowing he'd likely hear about being a few minutes late from his manager, Phil, Alex punched in.

5:37 p.m.

As Alex came out, he saw Turd hopping up and down, clutching his crotch.

"Really?" Alex said.

"You're killing me, Hanes," Turd said. He ran past him and blasted through the back room doors. "Watch the front!"

"You really ought to change your nickname," Alex called and shook his head, "for as much as you need to pee."

CHAPTER
3

Kevin Mustard was 17 and a junior at Alex's school, East Washburn High. No one ever called him Kevin though. His name was Turd to everyone in the world besides his parents and Phil, their manager. When Alex first started working with Turd a few months back, he read his nametag.

"Hey, what's up, Kevin? I'm Alex," he'd said.

"Okay, let's not get off on the wrong foot, bro," Turd had said. "Never mind what the nametag says. You don't call me Kevin. You call me Turd."

"Are you sure?" Alex asked. He wondered if the guy was messing with him, but Turd was completely serious. Even back then Turd looked like he pulled his clothes out of a hamper, didn't bother combing his long "rock 'n' roll" hair and did as little as possible while on the clock.

"Oh, I'm sure," Turd replied. "Anything you want me to call you?"

"Alex is fine," Alex said. "I don't really have a nick—"

"I'll find one for you," Turd interrupted. "I'm the nickname master. You'll see. Besides, I can't just call you Alex. That's weak."

And so, Alex and Turd became nearly constant coworkers. They never saw much of each other at school, but they got along well enough at the Gas N' Grab. It amazed Alex how many people knew Turd and called him by his unfortunate nickname.

A few weeks back, a guy from school came in and called him "Poo" instead of his usual moniker. Turd politely asked him to step outside for a moment. After some shouting Alex couldn't clearly make out, he watched Turd smash the kid in the head with a bottle of blue windshield cleaner.

The guy ran off, and when Turd came back in, he held up the exploded and empty plastic bottle.

"Ring me up for a bottle of this, would you, Hanes?"

✦ ✦ ✦ ✦ ✦

The store was empty, but a couple of cars were out at the gas pumps. Alex watched them carefully. Most convenience stores had cameras that could record license plate numbers. Phil installed "dummy" cameras instead, thinking it would save money and deter drive-offs. It really meant anyone working had to keep their eyes on the cars and be quick to write down the license plate of anyone who tried to "gas n' go."

Alex heard the toilet flush, and a moment later Turd emerged from the back room, zipping up his pants.

Turd came behind the front counter area and looked up at the halo of cigarette cartons above their heads. As if on autopilot, he tore open cartons and filled the slots that needed topping off. Alex knew he'd lose interest in a few minutes and flip through the horror movie magazines near the front door instead.

"Okay, Hip-Hop. Why were you late?"

It had been months since Alex's first day and Turd still hadn't settled on a nickname for him. Even so, that didn't stop him from trying out new ones to see what would stick.

"Forget it, man. You'd never believe me," Alex replied, but he immediately regretted it.

If there was one thing he'd learned in his short time working with Turd, it was that the guy was nosy.

"You ain't getting off that easy, kid," Turd replied. He blew a long strand of hair away from his lip. Once the carton of menthols was empty, he fired the box into the garbage. "Let's hear it."

Alex drew in a deep breath, told the car at Pump 3 it could go ahead, and faced his coworker. Turd smirked and waited as if bracing for some ridiculous excuse.

"Well?"

Okay, Alex thought, *try this on for size.*

"I found something on my way here," Alex began. "And it changed the world."

"Nice," Turd said and his eyes widened. "You found the cure for cancer?"

Alex laughed, realizing how sappy what he had said sounded. He should've known Turd would make jokes about it. Alex's smile quickly dissolved as he thought again about the other world. It seemed real and awful, and it was back in his head in an instant. He flinched just thinking about what he'd seen.

"Not what I meant," Alex explained. "It might sound stupid, but I found this glass lens kind of thing. When I held it up to the sun, it made the world change."

Turd stared at Alex and said nothing. He crossed his arms in front of his chest and shook his head, slowly.

"Do I look like an idiot?"

Alex felt sure Turd didn't really want him to answer, so he kept quiet.

"What do you mean *change*?" Turd said, stepping closer. "That's one of the dumbest things I've ever heard."

So Alex explained how it had happened. How he'd cleaned the lens off, held it to the sun, and found himself in a world 20 times more horrible than the neighborhood where the Gas N' Grab sat.

The front door beeped as a middle-aged guy in pajama pants entered and headed to the milk coolers.

"Shut up, Hanes. You're seriously kidding me, right?" Turd looked somewhere on the verge of laughing out loud and getting really upset. Considering what Alex saw him do to people who made him mad, he hoped Turd would just laugh in his face.

"I'm seriously not," Alex said quietly. He rang the guy's milk up, asked him if he wanted a bag or his receipt, and then thanked him for coming in.

"Seriously not what?"

"I'm seriously not kidding you," Alex said and kept his eye on the Oldsmobile at Pump 5. He turned back to Turd, who seemed stunned, as if unaware how to respond or act. For as long as Alex knew Turd, this was a first.

The uncomfortable quiet felt endless.

Then Turd spoke.

"Okay. Show me."

CHAPTER
4

Turd didn't want to wait. He made Alex go and get the lens right then and there. Alex felt a nervous twist in his stomach as he unzipped his backpack's back pocket in the store's back room. He hoped the lens wasn't in there. He hoped he'd just imagined the whole thing. He hoped he wouldn't regret telling Turd about what happened.

Alex's fingers touched the heavy, warm glass and despair instantly washed through him. He took a deep breath and pulled the lens from the pocket. Alex pushed his way through the back room doors as Turd finished ringing up a pack of cigarettes and a string of scratch-off lottery tickets for a middle-aged woman.

"Okay, Dark Wizard," Turd said, "let's see the doohickey."

"Wait. Was that some racist thing you just said?" Alex said, eyebrows raised. "Dark Wizard? Why do I gotta be a *dark* wizard?"

"What? No," Turd said and shook his head. "Dark wizards are into evil stuff. You know, like this creepy world you claim you saw. I've got a couple black friends, so—"

"Turd," Alex interrupted, "I'm messing with you."

"That nickname won't work will it?"

"Nope," Alex said. "Nice try, though."

Turd sighed and smiled sheepishly. He pulled back his dirty brown hair and bound it into a ponytail with the black band he always wore around his wrist.

"All right, enough screwing around," Turd said. "Let's see it."

With some hesitation, Alex handed over the dark lens. In that instant he wished he'd smashed it when he had the chance. It felt wrong holding it and even more so handing it to someone like Turd.

"Whoa," Turd said, turning it over in his fingers. "Look at this thing."

Turd held up the lens and Alex nearly knocked it out of his hand, afraid his coworker would plunge them into a world of darkness and terror. Turd squinted and peered at the inscriptions along the rounded edges.

"What's this say?"

Alex shrugged. "How should I know? I'm barely getting a C in Spanish. You think I can read those creepy etchings?"

Turd ignored Alex and pressed his palm flat against the surface of the lens.

"Man, was this in your pocket or something? It's warm."

Alex shook his head. "It was warm when I found it," he explained. He stepped over to the microphone and instructed the old guy at Pump 1 to lift the handle to turn on the pump.

"All right," Turd said. "It's pretty cool. I can't even joke about it."

Good, Alex thought. *He believes me.*

"Told you," Alex said. "Now give it back."

Turd raised the lens high over his head. Even though Alex was tall for his age, Turd had him by a few years and a few inches.

"Not so fast, McGrabby," Turd snapped. "I said it's cool. I never said I believed you."

Alex felt his temper rise. He didn't like where this was going.

"Here's the thing, Turd," Alex said. "I don't care if you believe me or not."

"Yeah, you do."

"No, I don't," Alex fired back.

"I'll need to see this for myself, you know," Turd insisted. "I'm a huge horror movie guy. If this thing works like you say it does . . . "

"You don't want to go there," Alex said. He shook his head. "I'm not kidding, man."

"Maybe you are, maybe you're not," Turd replied. "The thing is, I don't know you that well, Hanes. You might just have a really warped imagination. Or maybe you're a really good liar. But part of me thinks you might be telling the truth. One way or another, I'm going to find out."

"I'm making it up," Alex said quickly. "I'm . . . I'm working on a short story for class. For Halloween. It's about an eye of evil and . . . "

"Funny," Turd said. "Put the sign on the door. We're going out back."

Alex felt the wind rush from his lungs. It was almost like Turd had gut-punched him without the punch.

"Turd, we can't do this," Alex pleaded. "I'm not playing."

Turd shrugged. "We don't have a choice, Hanes. You started it."

"For real, man."

"PUT THE SIGN ON THE DOOR!"

Turd looked like he wanted to reach for a roll of quarters from the safe and sock Alex in the mouth. Wishing he'd just let the guys at the end of Third Street mug him, Alex fished around behind the plastic bags and found the WE'LL BE RIGHT BACK sign. It had a small clock with movable red hands that let customers know when they could expect the employees to open the store back up.

"What about the gas?" Alex knew they couldn't leave the store unattended and not watch the parking lot. He nodded toward the empty row of gas pumps.

"It'll be pay at the pump for a few minutes," Turd replied. "It's fine. We'll be right back."

Alex wondered if he could wrestle the lens from Turd's hands. If he could, Alex could run far enough away to take the lens and smash it to the ground. But if he couldn't, he might end up with a bottle of windshield washer fluid to the head.

Alex locked the front door and set the little clock for 10 minutes later. He pressed the small suction cups attached to each corner of the sign to the front door's glass. In the back of the store, Turd opened the door they used to toss trash into the Dumpster.

Here it goes, Alex thought. He tucked the keys to the store in his front pocket and headed for the back door.

CHAPTER
5

Outside, Alex saw Turd sitting on the old picnic table Phil put behind the store. Between the smell from the Dumpster and the cigarette butts all over the ground, Alex wasn't a bit surprised that very few people used it to actually picnic.

"Okay, Hanes," Turd said, hopping down. "How's this work?"

Alex considered making up something, but he knew Turd wasn't nearly as dumb as his nickname.

"I just held it up to the sun," Alex explained, miming the way he did it with his hands. "You sort of line it up so that the sun fits inside it or whatever."

Turd flipped the lens in his hand. Alex secretly prayed he would miss it and let it smash to the ground. But Turd played drums for the rock band Corpse Blaster in his spare time. He caught the lens without looking.

Alex watched.

"Like this?" Turd held it up with one hand, aiming it toward the sun. Alex cringed, almost expecting to see a purplish beam of light wash over Turd. It didn't.

"See?" Alex said. He reached for the lens. "It doesn't really work. I just made it all up."

Turd acted as if Alex hadn't said a thing. "Wait. I didn't line it up right."

"No, you did," Alex insisted. "It's not working, I guess."

"Bull. You're lying to me," Turd said as he tossed the lens back. Alex caught it, marveling again at its warmth. He thought about turning around, going back into the store and pretending he didn't hear his stubborn coworker.

"Let's forget it, Turd," Alex pleaded. "This is stupid."

"Just make it work, man," Turd said. "Real quick. We'll go in and back out again. We can do that, right?"

Alex paused and knew it was a moment too long. He let Turd know he was considering it. In that moment, he thought about how he'd gone over the first time and how easily he'd gotten back. He could do the same thing.

In and out. Real quick.

At least it would get Turd to shut up about it.

"Okay," Alex said. "I'm not sure if it'll bring both of us over or not, but get over here."

"Wait," Turd said. "You've got the keys, right?"

"Yeah." Alex patted his pocket. The Gas N' Grab lanyard hung from his shorts.

Turd ran over to the propped-open back door and knocked the wooden wedge loose from the bottom. The door swung closed with a slam, locking with a click.

"Gotta lock up," Turd mumbled.

"We're seriously going to go there and come right back," Alex said. "Not even five seconds."

"Yeah, yeah," Turd said. He stood close to Alex, almost too close. Turd smelled like corn chips.

"Let's see what happens," Alex said. He lifted up the lens, holding it above the two of them. Both boys looked up into the smoke-colored glass as Alex positioned it closer to the sun. Four of the carvings along the edge lit up.

"Whoa," Turd said. "It's working."

The remaining etchings ignited, and in seconds a wave of smoky light enveloped them. In one moment Alex saw the trees against the bright blue sky, and the next . . .

✦ ✦ ✦ ✦ ✦

. . . he was looking at the blackened skeleton of a tree against a deep red sky.

Immediately Alex could feel the heat and the stink of the other side. The scenery had changed since the last time he was there. A small, worn-down old hut stood where a house and garage used to be.

"Unreal," Turd gasped. He sounded like he was wincing and whispering at the same time. He took a cautious step forward, as if he meant to explore. His eyes were glued on the ramshackle structure ahead.

Ghostly faces and limbs peered and reached out from a windowless opening.

"Okay, man," Alex said. "We're going back. Right now."

"Wait," Turd said, taking another step. As he did, a gray, mottled tentacle shot through the dry, dead grass beneath his feet. It wrapped around his ankle.

"Hey, man!" Turd shouted, kicking with his free foot. Alex dashed forward and squatted near the thick appendage. He could see bugs swarming over the decomposed skin, yet the thing was still alive.

With the lens in his hand, he brought his fist down hard, cleaving some of the meat from the tentacle. It loosened its grip, and Turd stepped away.

"You see that?"

"Yes!" Alex shouted, standing up. "Now let's get out of here!"

Turd didn't have to be told twice, but he kept staring back at the ghoulish faces watching him from afar. Alex pulled his coworker so that they stood side by side. As he raised the lens, he swore he saw Turd nodding.

Doesn't matter, Alex thought. *We're out.*

The lens lit up and in moments . . .

✦ ✦ ✦ ✦ ✦

. . . they were back.

"No way!" Turd shouted. "That was unbelievable!"

"Yeah," Alex said. "You almost got us killed. Thanks for that."

Alex turned to the store, sufficiently angry. They needed to open up again. Who knew how many people had come up to see the

CLOSED sign? If Phil caught wind of what they'd done, they'd lose their jobs.

Alex reached into his front pocket for the keys . . . that weren't there.

"Seriously?" he whispered, turning both of his front pockets inside out. There was nothing in there except for his cell phone. "Turd, did I give you the keys?"

Turd was still carrying on, cheering to no one about what he'd seen.

"Turd! Do you have the keys?"

"No, man, you got 'em," Turd replied. He turned to look at Alex. "Don't you?"

Alex searched his pockets one last time along with the area where they'd stood. He even looked beneath the worn old picnic table.

The keys were gone.

CHAPTER
6

Turd didn't seem to be too upset about the keys. Alex was beside himself.

"You're getting way too crazy about this, man," Turd said. "It's simple. Give me the lens. I'll pop back over, scoop up the keys, and come right back. Piece of cake."

Alex looked at his coworker and instantly knew that wasn't what would happen. Turd seemed seduced by the other side. Alex knew if he let Turd go alone, he'd take his sweet time coming back.

If he ever came back at all.

"Maybe there's a spare key somewhere," Alex said, looking around. "One of those key rocks or something."

Turd laughed. "This isn't like some forgetful old lady's house," he said. "This is a place of business. There are thousands of dollars' worth of cigarettes hanging above the counter, and who knows the value of the other junk in there? Phil didn't just leave a spare key in case we jumped to a different world and left the store keys behind."

Alex hated being laughed at but knew Turd was right. They were locked out. If he wanted to keep his job, he'd have to go back.

"Fine," Alex said. "But I'll go. You should go around front and tell anyone waiting there that we'll be open in a couple of minutes."

Turd nodded. "Yeah, okay. Sure."

He took a step toward the side of the store as Alex raised the lens. Once the symbols lit up, Turd ran over to Alex, nearly knocking him over. Before Alex could stop it, the dark lens bathed them both in the smoky light once again. The world was at one instant bright and the next . . .

✦ ✦ ✦ ✦ ✦

. . . something darker and more twisted. The early evening sky became a darker red than before, and the clouds scattered across the horizon were thicker and black. Nearby houses were again replaced with hollowed-out hovels.

The lens fell from Alex's hand and Turd scooped it up. For the moment, Alex didn't care about that. He scanned the ground for the bright blue lanyard and the Gas N' Grab keys.

There.

The keys were lying in the straw-like dead grass, just inches from the hole where the rotten tentacle had emerged. Alex cautiously crouched down and grabbed them, expecting the diseased appendage to attack again.

"Got them," Alex whispered, almost as if declaring victory over the dark side.

He stood up and saw Turd staring at the haunted beings dwelling inside the old shack once again. Their miserable, pale faces had dark empty sockets where eyes belonged. Their mouths hung open, and ghastly moans echoed from their tortured throats.

"They want something," Turd whispered. The dark lens was still clutched in his hand, but he wore a stunned expression on his face.

"I got the keys. Let's get out of here," Alex warned. "Give me the lens, Turd!"

But Turd acted as if he hadn't heard a thing Alex said. He walked forward in a daze through a twisted mess of wrought iron until he was closer to the flimsy hut that penned the ghastly beings inside.

Their moans grew louder with every step he took.

"I hear their voices," Turd stammered. "They're calling to us."

Alex glanced over his shoulder to see the Gas N' Grab was now a pyre where the charred remains of things not-quite human smoldered. The acrid and sweet stink of melted flesh forced Alex to shield his nose with his arm.

We have to get back, Alex thought as his heart and mind raced with fear. *We got what we needed.*

Alex stepped over a black mass on the ground that shifted and moved suddenly. A tail swished back and forth as the shadowy creature disappeared beneath a mound of debris.

"Turd!"

Alex looked up in time to see his coworker reach toward the window where the tortured, groaning faces awaited.

"We have to free them," Turd murmured as Alex got closer. Turd had nearly reached inside the empty window when Alex grabbed his wrist. Turd jolted as if slapped across the face.

"We need to go!" Alex shouted. Further off in the world, the horizon rumbled and shrieks pealed through the wasteland. The ground trembled again. Alex feared it was the sound of heavy footsteps.

Giants, maybe, Alex thought, imagining what it could be based on the things he'd seen his first time around.

"They need our help," Turd whispered, reaching again for the hovel. Again, he acted as if he was in a trance.

Forget this, Alex thought. He grabbed for the lens.

Turd swung his arm up in defense, launching the glass piece over the other side of the dilapidated structure. Alex watched the dark lens disappear somewhere on the other side of the roof. Nausea and despair slipped through him in waves.

"Why did you do that, man?" Turd looked at Alex with bewildered eyes, his gaze broken. He grasped Alex by his Gas N' Grab vest just as the sound of splintering wood snapped behind them. In seconds, seven of the tortured beings tumbled out and onto the ground. Their skin looked pale and bruised in the faded light.

Alex watched in horror as the ghouls slowly rose to their feet. Both he and Turd instinctively turned toward the back door of the Gas N' Grab. They were faced with the blackened stack of bodies where the convenience store once stood.

"We have to get the lens back!" Alex screamed.

Over his coworker's shoulder, he saw the ghouls edge closer. Their arms were outstretched, and their mouths hung open, letting their constant moans escape more easily.

As the creatures staggered forward, Alex shoved Turd toward where a street once was in their world. In its place was a dried riverbed. Together they ran, leaving the mob of moaners behind. Even so, the ghouls turned and slowly stumbled in the boys' direction.

"The lens landed around back," Alex cried, nudging Turd toward the back of the old shack. The lens had flown over the top of the roof. Alex guessed it had landed somewhere nearby. When they rounded the shack's corner,

Alex saw something that made his heart nearly seize.

"A swamp," Turd blurted. "You think it's . . ."

Alex didn't hear the rest. He only stared, nearly frozen in disbelief.

CHAPTER
7

"That stupid thing is in there, isn't it?" Turd screeched. "Isn't it? We're gonna be stuck here!"

The swamp was a grayish mass of sludge that looked as thick as oatmeal. Blackened vegetation surrounded it, as thorny and deadly as everything else in this world. A bubble rose and broke at the surface, making Alex wonder what lurked beneath.

Knowing they were being followed and that there wasn't much time, Alex walked to the edge of the swamp.

"Maybe it's on the surface!" Alex cried. "The water is pretty thick. Maybe if it fell in here, it didn't sink!"

Turd stood beside him and pointed.

"Aw, man," Alex muttered. He saw the slot-shaped hole in the muck's surface Turd had spotted.

"I'm not getting in there," Turd insisted. "I'm a terrible swimmer."

Alex looked around, hoping beyond hope to find the lens somewhere at the edge of the swamp or in the brambles. He didn't see it.

The groaning of the slow-moving moaners grew louder. They were getting nearer. Then from above, the boys heard a screech as a black-winged beast dove from the sky, plucking up one of the ghouls with its twisted claws.

"Holy . . . " Alex began, watching the sky. The flying monster jerked its long neck back, flipping the ghoul into the air. It lunged forward, cleaving the moaner in half. The winged beast caught the meaty trunk in its jaws and let the legs fall. The severed appendages fell into the swamp with a wet *plop*.

Great, Alex thought. *God only knows what else is in that awful swamp.*

"I'll hold them off!" Turd cried. He picked up a wet piece of decimated wood and swung it behind them. Alex saw Turd connect with one of the moaners with a wet smack. The creature staggered a few steps but steadied itself.

"Fine," Alex said. "You keep your eye on me. I'll go in and see if I can find that thing."

Turd cracked another ghoul in the neck. This one, a woman, howled even louder. "These things are gonna keep coming!"

"If I'm not back in like five minutes,
just, you know . . . wait longer," Alex
said sheepishly.

"Quit stalling, Hanes! Get that
stupid lens!"

Alex watched what was left of the
dismembered legs disappear into the muck.
If the swamp was anything like quicksand,
he was in trouble. Figuring that there were a
million other ways to die in the dark world,
Alex dove in.

The swamp felt like jumping into watery
mashed potatoes and smelled like wet garbage
and rotten meat. Alex immediately gagged and
feared he'd puke up his burrito at any moment.
Trying to swim was next to impossible. The
muck was too thick and held him like he was
stuck in the world's most rancid Jell-O mold.

He did his best to keep his head up in an
attempt to see where the slit in the surface was.

Alex kicked his legs to keep himself afloat, and his foot struck something solid.

No way, he thought, his hopes raised. *Did I just find it?*

Taking as much of the humid, acrid air as he could into his lungs, Alex dove beneath the muck. As he kicked down, he realized that the swamp's surface was the thickest part. The water below was thick, but swimmable. He kept his eyes closed and felt around at the bottom. His fingers brushed something hard. A rock. He reached over to the left and touched what could only be a rotten face.

Alex fought the urge to scream underwater and swam away instead. As he did, something clamped his ankle, holding him in place. Immediately, whatever it was that had him pulled him back down.

Through the murky waters, Alex heard something groan as he thrashed, desperate to escape. He tried swimming away but got nowhere fast. With a free hand, he touched the muddy bottom of the swamp. As he did, something vibrated near his fingers.

The lens?

Alex twisted and pawed along the floor until his hand closed around a smooth, round, familiar shape. As he felt what little air he had escape his lungs, he swung the lens down on the tattered hand clutching his ankle.

The swamp creature groaned and loosened its grip. Alex balled himself up, then extended, freeing himself from the monster's grasp, and darted up through the viscous swamp muck.

As soon as his head crested, Alex drew in mouthfuls of the awful air. He coughed and spit as he struggled to catch his breath. With a slop-covered arm, he slapped away some of the swamp slime to get his bearings. He was near the middle of the sludge. Bubbles rose to the surface.

Whatever lurked down below was
rising up.

Alex kicked his legs as hard as he could
and used his arms to chop through the surface
muck, knocking thick splatters everywhere.
It worked, and he quickly carved his way
through the water until he reached the edge.

Like a slime-covered sailor who'd been
marooned at sea, Alex crawled on hands
and knees through the sickly looking brush.
Something behind him gurgled, but just then
Alex didn't care. He'd found the dark lens. He
and Turd could finally get their stupid butts
back home.

Alex looked up just as Turd kicked one of
the moaners in the gut. He followed it up with
a sharp crack to the head with the timber. He
almost looked like he was having fun.

"You get it?"

Alex stood up. The swamp slop fell off of him in quick, wet plops. He coughed and spit something to the ground. He patted his front pocket, too. The keys to the store were jammed down deep. He wouldn't lose them again.

"I got it," Alex gasped. The troublesome glass felt warm, heavy and yet oddly welcome in his hand. "Now let's get out of here."

CHAPTER
8

Alex actually found it difficult to pull Turd away from the cluster of moaners that seemed determined to get them. He watched Turd raise the stick like a barbarian and bring it crashing down on their miserable skulls.

Turd looked like a warrior—a warrior in a pair of camouflaged shorts and a blue Gas N' Grab vest with a KEVIN nametag pinned to it.

"Let's go, Turd!" Alex shouted.

Up above, the black-winged thing screeched as if on the hunt for another meaty morsel. Alex yanked Turd by the arm. A second later, the creature's claw snapped at the space Turd once occupied.

"Whoa!" Turd cried. He dropped his weapon in disbelief. They sprinted along the dried riverbed. Behind them, the moaners staggered and regrouped from the thrashings Turd had delivered. In a blink, another ghoul was snapped up into the sky.

Alex looked around. There, in the spot where Joe's Burgery & Bar stood in their world, sat the remains of a ruined stone structure. A slab of stone left from the upper floor covered the lower like a post-apocalyptic cave. It would have to do.

"Come on!" Alex shouted. "We have to get somewhere safe and aim this thing at the sun!"

"Right," Turd replied, then added, "Oh, dude. You stink!"

They scrambled over a crumbled wall and into the hollowed-out shelter. Clustered in one corner of the building's remains sat a group of motionless skeletons. They looked like they had died huddled together, watching the horrors outside.

"Grim," Turd said, walking over to them. Alex watched, horrified, as he touched the top of the biggest skeleton's skull. As he did, the skull crumbled to dust.

"Really?" Alex asked. "You had to touch that dead guy's skull? What's wrong with you?"

Turd shrugged.

"Are we safe in here?" Alex asked, suddenly painfully aware of how bad he really *did* stink.

"Besides the Bones family over here? I think so," Turd replied. "For now."

Alex looked outside. Only one of the moaners still stumbled their way. If there was any luck in the dark world, Alex hoped the black-winged thing would snatch it up. He motioned for Turd to join him. Once together, Alex raised the lens to the sky.

Turd quickly asked the obvious question: "Where's the sun?"

Alex lowered the lens and scanned the dark red sky. Panic quickly rose within him as he noticed the sky was mostly overcast, choked with black clouds. The sun was nowhere to be found.

"You have to be kidding me," Alex whispered.

"Hold it up anyway," Turd suggested. "Maybe it'll still work."

Alex nodded. He aimed the lens toward the brightest patch of clouds, hoping it was enough. They huddled close to watch the symbols along the perimeter of the lens light up.

They never did.

"Great," Turd muttered. "This sucks."

Alex swore and slipped the lens into his front pocket. It felt like a warm weight against his damp leg.

"Once the clouds pass, we go," Alex said, watching the sky. There was little hope as the clouds didn't appear to be moving. With every passing moment, the sky grew even darker.

"Right, genius," Turd said, staring at the crimson heavens with him. "And when the sun sets?"

Alex felt like he'd been knifed in the heart. He blew air slowly though his teeth, thinking about what that meant. *Would the sun set? Would it rise again?* He couldn't imagine how terrifying the dark world would be once night fell.

The ground rumbled, as if reminding Alex that they weren't safe. Not by a long shot.

Alex studied the rest of the structure he and Turd hid in. They were totally exposed by the opening they'd entered through. If the sun didn't break out anytime soon, anything outside could trap them where they stood.

"We can't stay here," Alex said. "We should move before it's too late."

Turd put his hand to his head as if massaging a massive headache away.

"Seriously? Where are we gonna go?"

Alex didn't know, especially since things on the dark side were very different from their world. He scanned the horizon. Farther off to what might've been the north, a giant flesh golem tore into a hunk of mangled meat with twitching legs.

Not that way, Alex thought, turning his attention to the west.

There, where downtown existed in his world, stood a cluster of hollowed-out towers, looking more like the ruins of a city than anything else. Even so, the structures looked mostly intact.

"Maybe downtown," Alex replied finally. "Get inside somewhere and hide. Everything here seems too wide open. The little structures are flimsy, too."

Turd whistled, looking in the direction Alex indicated.

"Dang," Turd blurted. "Makes me wonder what downtown will be like."

"And it'll be a long walk . . . or run." Alex said. He brushed away some swamp slop that clung to his clothes. He wasn't sure why, but he even wiped his nametag clean.

From somewhere closer than Alex cared for, something being terrorized or torn apart shrieked. What followed was a wet, mashing sound. The two Gas N' Grab employees looked at each other.

"We should go," Turd said.

CHAPTER
9

Alex had walked downtown from his house hundreds of times in the real world. If he didn't mess around, and wasn't mugged, it usually took him around 45 minutes. In a dark world populated with awful things, traveling took a lot longer.

As the sky grew dimmer by the moment, Turd verbalized something Alex had just noticed himself.

"Time moves quicker here."

It was true. What was probably sometime after 6:00 in their world felt like 9:00 where

they were now. What they saw of the sun
quickly disappeared in the scarred horizon.

Alex tried the dark lens again and
again, hoping there was enough sunlight
peeking behind the clouds to illuminate
all of the symbols. There wasn't. The sun
weakened by the moment, threatening to
disappear completely.

When the sun finally did disappear,
covering them in night, a chill ran through
Alex's bones. Where the day was hot and
humid, the night had become cold. A wind
blew through the black void, making Alex's
soggy shorts ripple.

"We need to find some light," Turd said.
He fished out his cell phone and pressed the
center button. It cast a weak white glow that
didn't do much but light up his face.

Alex did the same and for the first time
noticed strange symbols and patterns covering

his phone's home screen. He wiped some of the swamp muck from the waterproof case.

"Is your phone doing weird stuff?"

"Yeah," Turd said. "But then again, my phone drops calls all the time anyway. I'm not surprised."

Alex wondered how soon they'd run into something awful and hungry in the dark. Off in the distance, a fire burned away at something. Though he couldn't see the city in the dark, it appeared to be in the same direction.

"Over there," Alex whispered.

Eager to escape the dark, they headed toward the fire. As they did, Alex heard what sounded like small footsteps moving toward them. A moment later, Turd cried out in pain as if some creature had attacked him. A snarl in the dark confirmed it.

"What?" Alex shouted. "What happened?"

"Oh, man," Turd cried. "Something got me, Alex. I . . . "

Alex felt his pulse race, and his instinct to avoid danger jumped into overdrive. He grabbed Turd, finding his work vest in the dark, and tugged. As he did, Turd cried out again.

"That thing bit me, man!" Turd blurted. "Took a chunk out of my arm!"

"Can you run?" Alex asked. "If your legs work, we gotta move, T!"

They sprinted to the fire and Alex heard the thunder of small footsteps just behind them. He didn't dare look back, worried instead about what was ahead. For now, the fire was a beacon, a possible oasis. He just hoped it wouldn't lead them to more trouble.

"It's right behind us!"

"Shut up and run!" Alex shouted.

When they finally reached the fire, Alex couldn't tell what the flames were burning. It looked like some sort of metal, box-shaped contraption. The bottom looked like a gigantic fridge with strange, blackened metal appendages attached to it.

Right away, Alex scanned the small, lit-up circle the fire created. The carcass of something green and scaly laid on its side. The eyes had been eaten from the lizard-thing's face and the mouth gaped open to reveal rows of small but sharp teeth.

"Hey, man," Turd said, holding his arm. "I'm bleeding pretty bad!"

The wound on Turd's bicep was decent sized. Blood dribbled from it and onto his hand. Alex glanced behind them, edging closer to the fire. Whatever it was that chased them waited in the dark.

Something doesn't like the light, Alex understood quickly.

Off in the distance, a huge roar rumbled the ground as if giant footsteps were falling. Alex took a deep breath and quickly prayed they weren't the ones to anger such an enormous beast.

"We have to find a way to bring fire with us to the city," Alex said quickly. "Whatever chased us doesn't like it."

Turd stood silent, doing nothing to help. Or so Alex thought.

"Is that lizard thing stiff?"

"How should I know?" Alex snapped, eyes widened in irritation. "And who cares if—"

"Kick it real quick," Turd ordered.

Alex did as he was told. "Yeah. It's like petrified. Great."

Turd winced as he moved his hand to point. Blood dripped from his finger.

"Grab some of those dry weeds and stuff it in that thing's mouth," Turd said.

"I don't think—"

"Just do it," Turd said, interrupting him. "We can use it for a torch."

Alex wasn't thrilled with the idea of touching the thorny-looking weeds, let alone the lizard carcass, but there wasn't much choice. He quickly snatched up some of the driest foliage and jammed it into the lizard's open jaws.

Before he could talk himself out of it, Alex picked up the dead reptile and poked the head into the flames. In seconds, he had a makeshift torch.

"Nice," Turd said with a grunt. He clutched his arm again to stop the blood from flowing.

"Any ideas on how to whip together a first aid kit?"

"Funny," Turd said. "Let's move before your fire burns out."

Alex didn't need to be told again. He held onto the thick tail of his lizard torch, lighting the way. As they made their way through the darkness, creatures skittered out of their path. A humanoid figure that looked sewn together from various scraps of meat staggered backward, its arms outstretched to keep the light off of it. The creature fell backward, groaning.

While the torch cleared the way to the edge of the city for Alex and Turd, anything with eyes now knew exactly where they were.

CHAPTER
10

Half of the lizard had burned away
by the time Alex and Turd reached the
city. Small fires burned in the gutted-out
ruins of the city, casting light on what was left
of the buildings. Hunks of crumbled concrete
made jagged piles. Somewhere in the dark, it
sounded like someone was weeping.

Alex noticed the structures looked older,
rustic and constructed of worn, chiseled stone.
Some of the structures seemed as tall as their
counterparts in his world but had an ominous
feel to them.

As they slipped between the towers, they searched for one that could provide some protection. Alex knew they had to get through the night and into morning.

Many of the entrances were sealed with ironclad doors, bolted shut from the inside. Alex wondered who or what was locked in there. They moved on. As the lizard torch burned dangerously close to the tail, Turd piped up.

"What's all that smoke?"

Alex noticed it seemed hazier, too. But not from the fire he carried. The air looked dustier here. When he lowered the light to his feet, Alex saw what it was.

Ash.

He kicked his foot through the thin layer. His shoe knocked something loose and he watched a jawbone tumble through the pale dust.

"Let's get inside," Alex decided. "Now."

Ahead stood a tower with a door hanging open. Alex pulled it open further, making it groan on rusty hinges and likely alerting everything to their presence. Both boys slipped inside and tugged the heavy door closed behind them.

"There's a latch," Turd said. "Move the light over here."

Alex did and together they slid the rough metal bolt across and into the frame. Nothing would get inside.

The tower's lower level was mostly empty. The light revealed an overturned table, chunks of rock and random pieces of wood. Alex was sure whatever had happened to the city had affected the tower, too.

"Stairs," Turd said. "We should go up."

Alex agreed and they climbed a wooden stairwell that never seemed to end. The wooden stairs creaked. The steps were gritty and loud beneath their shoes. Their footsteps scraped and echoed in the dark. After what seemed like 20 or more floors, Alex found a door.

"This is high enough," Alex whispered.

Turd grimaced in agreement.

The two of them emerged onto a vacant floor. Things were scattered around, abandoned by whatever had occupied the space before: a rusty pail, a few carved sticks that may have been weapons, and an old lantern.

To be safe, Alex closed the door behind them.

"This will have to do," Alex said. He walked around the entire open space and found no interior walls. Where windows should've been, square holes looked out into the black. There wasn't a pane of glass in any of them.

The floor was empty. The two of them were alone.

"Your torch is almost out," Turd said from his spot on the ground. He sat and held his wounded arm.

Alex found a heap of rags piled in the corner. As he drew closer, he realized it was a dead woman, long since rotted away, lying facedown on the floor.

He held his breath and tugged at her tattered outer jacket. It came away easily as her arms separated from her torso and quickly crumbled to ash. A moment later, the rest of her body disintegrated.

"Wow," Alex said. He stuffed the coat into the rusty bucket and touched the remnants of the torch to the fabric. In moments, they had a small, portable fire pit.

"Should've grabbed some marshmallows back at the store," Turd said when Alex finally sat down.

"Yeah," Alex said. "Wait here. I'll go get some and come back."

Turd laughed as Alex studied his coworker's condition. He looked pale, making Alex wonder how bad the wound really was. It still appeared to be bleeding, so Alex shrugged off his work vest and tore it in two.

"Phil's going to kill you," Turd said.

"I'm not too worried about Phil right now, you know?" Alex said. He squatted near Turd and motioned for him to raise his arm. Once he did, Alex wrapped the strap of vest fabric around the wound. For good measure, he used his Gas N' Grab employee nametag to pin it in place.

"Tight enough?"

"Yeah," Turd mumbled, touching it a bit. "It's good."

The two of them sat in silence for a moment, watching the open windows. The only sound they heard was the wind whipping through the openings. It made Alex feel somewhat safer.

Just until the sun comes up, Alex thought. He just prayed the morning wouldn't be overcast like tonight was. He couldn't even see the moon.

He touched the heavy dark lens in his pocket, reassuring himself that it was still there.

"We should sleep a little," Alex suggested.

"You're kidding, right?"

Alex shrugged, but Turd was right. Sleeping didn't sound like much of an option. He reached into his pocket and pulled out the dark lens. In the flickering light of the bucket fire, Alex studied the cursed object.

"Why'd you ever pick up that thing?" Turd asked.

Alex also wondered why he even bothered to keep it. Especially after his first brief trip to the dark side.

"Not sure," Alex whispered.

They sat and talked for what seemed like hours, silencing themselves anytime they thought they heard a noise in their refuge for the night.

When they finally felt comfortable and safe, the creatures appeared.

CHAPTER
11

Turd heard them first. He stood up and covered his bandaged arm with his hand as if to protect it. Alex looked to where Turd stared and saw it. There, in the open glassless window of their hiding spot, crouched a shadowy figure. It was black and sleek, nearly camouflaged by the night. It looked ready to pounce on them at any moment.

The thing's eyes shimmered in the flickering light. Somewhere in its throat came a distinct clicking sound. Moments later, more appeared in the other nearby windows. They crowded the openings, watching Alex and Turd. Before long, the clicking sound multiplied and grew louder.

They're calling for more to join them, Alex thought. He stood up slowly and considered moving out of the light. Somehow he was certain the creatures would see him no matter where he went.

"We better think of something fast," Turd whispered. "This is the part in horror movies where we die."

"Shut up," Alex whispered. He still held the lens in his hand, knowing it wasn't much of a weapon. He also knew he couldn't risk dropping and breaking it. Somehow he forgot to slip it back into his pocket.

Turd stood and looked along the ground as if to find something to fight with. Alex scolded himself for not bringing along the pieces of wood he'd seen earlier.

"Maybe if you didn't stink so bad they wouldn't have found us," Turd whispered.

"They probably smell your blood," Alex snapped back, "and want more."

The creatures seemed to pay no mind to the bickering but watched the boys with wet, expressionless eyes. Alex moved his hand a bit, angling the lens toward the bucket fire.

And then something unexpected happened.

A small, orange beam burst from the front of the lens. A jagged orange line burned into the dusty concrete floor, six inches from the pail. Smoke rose from the glowing slash the lens created.

"Did you see that?" Turd shouted.

The dark lens vibrated in Alex's hand, and then the creatures pounced.

The room became a frenzied blur of black shapes surging forward. Turd kicked, catching one of the creatures in the teeth. Its shiny black head snapped back as it growled in pain. Alex turned the front of the lens to the creature, slashing the monster across the chest. A second later, it fell into two gory heaps. Dead.

Another creature dove for Alex, and he tilted the lens upward. The orange light sliced the creature's head in half, splitting it like a melon.

"Keep doing that!" Turd shouted. "They're still coming!"

Alex saw Turd briefly wrestle with one. He screeched in pain as the monster grasped his wounded arm. With amazing precision, Alex burned off the creature's arm. Turd wasted no time in snatching up the arm and smacking the creature across the face with it. When the creature staggered back from the blow delivered from its severed arm, Alex finished the job.

Even so, more lurkers came.

We're good as long as the fire keeps burning, Alex thought. He made short work of three more of the monsters scrambling across the floor. The windows were still cluttered with the creatures, so much so that he couldn't see outside.

Alex crouched to get closer to the fire. When he did, the size of the orange beam grew in diameter and the dark lens vibrated even harder in his hand. He swung the beam back and forth across the floor, making sure to keep it clear of Turd. As he did, he heard the creatures screech and drop. Chunks of the outer wall melted and crumbled away, exposing their lofty battleground to the night. It was then that Alex saw something glorious.

The rising sun.

More creatures climbed up from the lower floors. Some tried to sneak up on Alex from the side, but he saw them coming. He steered the beam to them, quickly slaughtering the monsters.

The floor was covered with piles of dismembered bodies. Alex had no idea how many creatures there were or how many more were coming. They had to escape!

"Turd!" Alex cried. The sun continued to rise over the horizon. "Get over here!"

His coworker slammed the severed arm down on the head of a crouched creature, pulverizing the fiend. He skittered over to Alex.

"I've never been so happy to see a sunrise," Turd cried, getting as close to Alex as either of them could stand.

Alex raised the lens toward the light, hoping the morning sun was enough to activate the inscriptions. He saw at least a dozen creatures dash to tear them apart and prayed their return would be fast enough.

"Hang on!" Alex cried as the symbols along the edge of the smoky glass lit up. He saw a blinding white light and . . .

✦ ✦ ✦ ✦ ✦

. . . Alex heard Turd say something his mom would've been angry to hear coming from his own mouth. He opened his eyes to see they were inside a building. There were cubicles around them. A guy with a vacuum and a gray mustache stared at them like they just appeared from nowhere.

Which they had.

"Where are we?" Turd asked.

Alex realized they were in some sort of office building after hours. The guy from the cleaning crew was their biggest clue.

"I don't know how you got in here, but you guys need to leave," the older man said after shutting off his vacuum cleaner. "Now."

"We're gone, sir," Turd said. "Thank you."

Alex slipped the lens into his pocket as he and Turd headed for the elevator. They took it to the bottom floor. The night security guard at the front desk gave them a confused look as they stepped out into the city. Above the buildings, the moon was bright and full.

"We're probably fired. You know that, right?" Turd said. He looked at his bandaged arm and shook his head.

"Yeah," Alex said. "But I blame you. You just had to see it for yourself."

"I don't care," Turd said. "That place sucked anyway."

"Which? The Gas N' Grab or the other place?"

"Both," Turd said. "But I never liked working at the Gas N' Grab."

Alex nodded. So it would take him longer to get his car now that he was likely unemployed. He had bigger things to worry about just then. Like getting Turd to the hospital to have his arm looked at.

He just hoped they didn't get mugged along the way.

"You ever going to throw the thing away?" Turd asked. "After all the trouble it's caused?"

Alex removed the lens from his pocket. He turned it in his hand once and then tossed it into an overflowing garbage can as they passed by. It landed amid a discarded newspaper and a sack of fast-food wrappers.

"There," Alex said. "Gone."

Turd stopped at the can, staring at the lens. Alex could tell by the look on Turd's face that he was up to something.

"Leave it, man," Alex said. "We need to get you to the hospital."

"Yeah, yeah," Turd said, letting go of his arm for a moment. He reached down and plucked the lens out of the garbage can. "Just want to hold it one last time."

Alex sighed, remembering how the lens had drawn him in when he found it. It made him wonder what happened to the person who had it before him.

"Okay, let's get—"

✦ ✦ ✦ ✦ ✦

Without warning, Turd held the lens up to the moonlight. Alex saw the symbols along the edge light up and just like that, Turd was . . .

"Gone," Alex whispered.

About the Author

Thomas Kingsley Troupe has always written stuff. Well . . . at least since he was in second grade. Back then it was comic books starring stick people and spaceships. Later it was horror tales and twisted Christmas stories that pretty much ruined the holidays. He also dabbled in writing and directing short films that had audiences laughing one minute and feeling sick another. These days he's the author of more than 50 books for kids. When he's not writing stories, he's fighting fires and hunting ghosts as an investigator with the Twin Cities Paranormal Society. He lives in Woodbury, Minnesota, where he chases his ~~boys~~ monsters around the house. Visit him online at www.thomaskingsleytroupe.com.

Questions to Think About

1. Imagine you are Alex. Would you have told Turd about the dark lens? Why or why not?

2. When Alex uses the lens to go back into the strange world to get the keys he dropped, why do you think Turd goes back with him?

3. On the other side of the dark lens is a dark and dangerous world. How do you think it got that way? Write a story about what this world and its people were once like, and then describe the event or events that changed everything.

4. At the end of the story, Turd holds up the lens to the moon. When the lens is held up to the sun, the person holding it is transported to a grim, fiery world. Where do you think Turd went when he held up the lens to the moon? Write a story about it.

THE ALABASTER RING

When Ethan receives a box of his dad's old belongings, what he finds puts him at odds with a killer from an international crime organization. Will Ethan and his new friend, Kendra, find what they are looking for before they come face to face with a criminal mastermind?

CONCRETE GALLERY

When Keena goes missing before her big art show, Xriss knows something is wrong. He follows clues to find her and quickly discovers that he's not the only one looking. Her abusive father and a local gang are both on her trail. Xriss needs to find Keena before it's too late.

WOLF HIGH

Nobody knows Alex's secret—not his teachers, not his best friend, Harry, not even the other werewolves at his school. Just his mom. That's because she helped create the drug that turned people into werewolves. Now she's trying to find a cure before Alex hurts someone . . . or worse.

READ MORE FROM 12-STORY LIBRARY

Every 12-Story Library book is available in many formats, including Amazon Kindle and Apple iBooks. For more information, visit your device's store or 12StoryLibrary.com.